GULP, GOBBLE

by Marilyn Singer
illustrated by Kathryn Durst

Ready-to-Read

SIMON SPOTLIGHT

An imprint of Simon & Schuster Children's Publishing Division • New York • London • Toronto • Sydney • New Delhi
1230 Avenue of the Americas, New York, New York 10020 • This Simon Spotlight edition September 2019
Text copyright © 2019 by Marilyn Singer • Illustrations copyright © 2019 by Kathryn Durst.
All rights reserved, including the right of reproduction in whole or in part in any form. SIMON SPOTLIGHT,
READY-TO-READ, and co   1c. For information about
special discounts for bulk   es at 1-866-506-1949 or
business@simonan   erica 0719 LAK
10 9 8 7 6 5 4 3 2 1   ress. LCCN 2019012496
ISBN 978-1-5344-2134   5344-2135-6 (eBook)

Here is a list of all the words you will find in this story and a guide on how to pronounce them. Sound the words out before you begin reading the story.

gulp	→	(guhlp)
gobble	→	(GAH-bull)
peck	→	(pehk)
pick	→	(pihk)
fish	→	(fihsh)
forage	→	(FORE-ij)
lap	→	(laap)
lick	→	(lihk)
graze	→	(grayze)
guzzle	→	(GUH-zull)
snap	→	(snaap)
slop	→	(slahp)

suck	→	(suhk)
swallow	→	(SWAH-lo)
crunch	→	(kruhnch)
crop	→	(krahp)
hook	→	(hook)
harvest	→	(HAR-vist)
sip	→	(sihp)
slurp	→	(slerp)
gnaw	→	(naw)
nibble	→	(NIH-bull)
browse	→	(browz)
burp	→	(berp)

Ready to go? Happy reading!

gobble,

peck,

pick.

Fish,

forage,

lap,

lick.

Graze,

guzzle,

snap,

slop.

Suck,

swallow,

crunch,

crop.

Hook,

harvest,

sip,

slurp.

Gnaw,

nibble,

browse . . .

burp!